Audrey
of the
Outback

Christine Harris

Illustrations by Ann James

LITTLE HARE
www.littleharebooks.com

Little Hare Books
8/21 Mary Street, Surry Hills
NSW 2010 AUSTRALIA

www.littleharebooks.com

First published in 2008

National Library of Australia
Cataloguing-in-Publication entry
Harris, Christine, 1955- .
Audrey of the outback.

For primary school children.
ISBN 978 1 921272 18 9.

1. Imagination - Juvenile fiction. 2. Country life - South
Australia - Juvenile fiction. I. Title. (Series : Harris,
Christine, 1955- Audrey of the outback).

A823.3

Cover design by Simon Rattray
Set in 13/18pt Stone Informal by Clinton Ellicott
Printed in Australia by Griffin Press, Adelaide

5 4 3 2 1

Audrey of the Outback

For Cianah, and Whitie,
who tripped over a rock—CH

For all of you who feel the past whispering
through the present; for Nikki who can do things
practical and magical; and for Marjie James's
grade in Robinvale—AJ

Audrey leaned further out.

One

Audrey Barlow parted the hessian curtains and leaned out of her bedroom window. Her fair plaits swung forward like heavy ropes.

'Stumpy,' she whispered. 'Quick, come here.'

She checked back over her shoulder. Douglas, her three-year-old brother, had 'sneaky feet'. At least, he did when he wore his kangaroo-skin slippers. When he walked over the skins spread across the mud floor he didn't make a sound. But he wasn't in the room.

Audrey leaned further out. When she was in a hurry, she was glad her parents couldn't afford glass. She could stick her head through the window quickly.

'This is our chance, Stumpy. We're going to find out the swagman's secret ...' She tilted her head, straining to hear Stumpy's soft words. 'What was that? Yes, it *is* a secret.'

The swagman had arrived the previous evening, just before the sun set. Swaggies turned up from time to time, hoping Mrs Barlow would give them flour or sugar. They didn't have houses of their own and slept outside under the stars. Most swaggies offered to work in exchange for food. But some arrived as the sun was going down and left early in the morning so they didn't have to do chores. Dad called those sort 'sundowners'.

This swaggie arrived just as the family was sitting down to kangaroo stew. The sudden knock on the door made Audrey squeal. Lightning, the blue heeler dog, used to announce visitors with his bark. But a month ago a snake bit him and now he was buried out the back.

Price leapt up to open the door to a swagman who was taller and more solid than anyone Audrey had ever seen. He blocked the doorway with his large body. His dark beard was bushy enough to make an eagle's nest. Years in the sun had pouched his eyes with wrinkles. His scuffed boots were dusty. Audrey noticed a split in the side seam of his brown jacket. He probably didn't have anyone to sew for him, and his own fingers looked too thick to hold a needle.

But it was not his size or his thick beard that made Audrey stare. It was the bulging chaff bag he carried. Swaggies always had their bedrolls strapped to their backs with a tea billy or saucepan hanging from it. But this bag was different. It bulged unevenly, with bits sticking out as though it was packed with fingers. And it rattled.

Audrey itched to know what was inside.

Now Audrey pleaded with Stumpy. 'You *have* to come with me to the swaggie's camp. Or I'll never sleep again. Last night my eyes kept popping open all by themselves.'

She couldn't get the rattle of that chaff bag out of her head. It made her shiver.

Two

Audrey skipped into the kitchen. A large yellow bowl on the bench hinted there might be cake later on. Sometimes Audrey was allowed to help by rubbing goat butter and flour together between her fingers. The goat butter smelt sour on its own, but not after it was cooked in a cake. Especially if her mum added spices from the little tins.

Mrs Barlow wiped her hands on her apron, leaving a smudge of flour. The flowery apron had faded patches and was darned with thread that did not match. But

Audrey thought the apron made her mum look pretty. The leaves around the little flowers brought out the green in her eyes.

Audrey's mum once told her, 'You've got my eyes.'

It made Audrey laugh. 'No, I haven't. You've still got your eyes. I can see them stuck in your head.'

Mrs Barlow handed Audrey a tin. 'Tell the man these are all the eggs we can spare for now.'

Audrey peeked inside. There were four eggs, nestled in bran to stop them rolling against each other.

'He said his name is Toothless,' Audrey reminded her mum.

Most swagmen were known by their nick-names. But Audrey couldn't work this one out. Yesterday, she had seen lots of teeth gleaming through the man's bushy beard. His teeth were as crooked as a dog's hind leg, but they were all there. The swagman was a mystery, all right.

Douglas ran into the kitchen and jumped into the air, fingers outstretched, trying to touch the dried apricots that hung on strings from the ceiling. But he had a lot of growing to do before he would reach them. Hanging dried fruit kept it away from ants. Flour and sugar bags were on big hooks for the same reason.

Mrs Barlow limped to a chair and sat down.

'Is your leg whingeing today, Mum?' asked Audrey.

Mrs Barlow shrugged. Douglas flung himself over her knees and she winced. 'Audrey, please don't earbash that poor swagman,' she said. 'You could talk the hind leg off a donkey.'

Audrey nodded and straightened her back so she would look taller. 'I'm nearly growed up.'

'Grown, with an "n".'

'Gwow-dup,' said Douglas, in a muffled voice, as though it was one long word. With his head dangling on one side of his mother's knees and his feet on the other, he was a talking seesaw.

'When you get back you can clean out the chookyard, Audrey,' said Mrs Barlow. 'It's your turn.'

Audrey frowned. The chooks were all right. And she liked eating their eggs. But she hated cleaning out the yard. It was smelly. And the manure had to be bucketed all the way to the vegetable patch. It was enough to put people off vegetables.

'I'll take Stumpy with me,' said Audrey.

'I thought you might.'

Carefully cradling the tin of eggs, Audrey stepped out of the kitchen into dazzling sunlight. She blinked as her eyes adjusted.

Her older brother, Price, still wasn't back from checking his traps. He must have caught lots of rabbits.

Stumpy was waiting at the back door. He looked as though he was sulking, but Audrey knew he didn't mean it. Stumpy hated waiting around for her to come outside. She smiled to show she was glad he was coming along too.

Buttons, one of the goats, bleated. Audrey had named her Buttons because she had been 'cute as a button' when she was small. Now she had the same wobbly ears and knobby knees as Sassafras, the mother goat.

'You can't be hungry again, Buttons,' said Audrey. 'All you do is eat.'

Audrey walked between the chookyard and the long-drop dunny. She crossed the red sandy clearing that separated the house from the scrub. Her dad had insisted on a wide clearing for a firebreak.

'Hello, Pearl. Hello, Esther,' she called out as she passed the wooden crosses that marked her sisters' graves.

Stumpy never spoke to them. He hadn't known Pearl and Esther.

There was a path, worn by camels and the occasional horse and cart. But it was quicker to cut through the scrub to the swaggie's camp. There was a permanent clearing near a dry creek bed, where swagmen usually stayed. A pile of grey ashes marked where they built their camp fires. It was a nice shady spot to camp.

Audrey had secret cubbyhouses nearby, but there was no time to play. She had to deliver the eggs without breaking them. And then she was going to find out what that swagman had in his chaff bag.

Three

The day was quickly warming up.

'By this afternoon it'll be hot enough to fry an egg in the sand,' Audrey told Stumpy.

He made a face. Stumpy didn't like eggs, whether they were fried or not.

Overhead a wedge-tailed eagle circled. Brown, with white markings, the eagle seemed to drift lazily on the wind. But Audrey knew that eagles had keen eyes. They could see the smallest mouse or skink running through the grass.

Audrey balanced the tin of eggs on one

hand and curled the other around her mouth. 'Cooee!'

Her call resounded through the trees. She imagined the sound shaking birds from their nests, disturbing leaves and jostling clouds. She looked up. Actually, there were no clouds. But it was fun pretending.

'Cooee,' came an answering call.

A thin trail of smoke coiled above the trees.

'Stumpy,' Audrey said, 'you'd better stay here. You don't always behave.'

She took two steps, then hesitated. Again, she remembered the strange rattling that had come from the swagman's chaff bag. A tingle ran down her spine. 'Stumpy, if I call out, run in and get me, all right?'

Stumpy nodded.

Toothless sat on the ground beside a small fire. There was a lump of cooked damper in his hand. It was flatter than the damper Audrey's dad made. Dad added a pinch of carb soda to puff up the flour, which made the damper lighter, more like a scone.

Carefully, Audrey stepped over a line of ash from the fire. Putting hot ash around the camp was supposed to keep ants away. The idea was that they wouldn't want to burn their little anty feet. It didn't work for long, though. Ash soon cooled.

Dad sometimes said, 'You kill a hundred ants, and another five hundred come to the funeral.'

The swagman's cheeks bulged with damper. His dark beard bounced up and down as he chewed. He nodded a greeting.

'I've brought your eggs, Mister Toothless,' said Audrey. 'Mum can only spare four. The chooks aren't laying properly since a fox got under the wire and ate some of them. They got a fright.'

The man swallowed. 'Just got one name. Toothless. There's no Mister.' He held up his damper. 'Eggs will make a nice change from this rock.'

Audrey smiled. So he wasn't much of a cook, then.

His nails were grubby. Out here, with little water and too much sand, it was impossible to keep clean.

She sat down, facing him. 'Do you reckon chooks just stop making eggs? Or do you think they're still in there and the chooks are holding on tight so they don't drop out?'

'Don't know the answer to that one,' said Toothless. 'But thank your mother for the eggs. Be down later to see if I can help her any.'

He wiped his mouth with the back of his hand. Damper crumbs fell from his beard. 'There's tea left in the billy. Want some?'

'Yes, please.' Audrey could stay longer if she had a drink, and it would be rude to say no.

Toothless reached over to search among his things.

The large chaff bag Audrey remembered from the night before rested beside his rolled blanket. Yesterday he had gripped the top of that bag as though he never wanted to let it go. Now, his elbow bumped against the bag and it rattled.

Audrey's stomach fluttered. She couldn't drag her eyes away from that bag. What was in there?

Her eyes slid again to the chaff bag.

Four

Toothless found a spare tin pannikin. He filled it with tea from his battered billy. Then he sat the billy back down on the coals.

The tea was black because the leaves had been brewing for some time. It would be strong and probably bitter. But Audrey took the pannikin with a smile of thanks.

Gingerly, she took a sip. The tea was strong, all right. But it had the smoky aroma of eucalyptus leaves that she liked. The metal pannikin was warm against her fingers.

'My dad's a dogger,' she told Toothless. 'He's away. Last trip, he sold five hundred dingo scalps to the government. So Mum says she wants real glass in the windows.'

Audrey liked dogs, but dingoes were different. They didn't bark, just howled. It was a sound that made you shudder at night. Dingoes attacked sheep and cows. Audrey's dad had once seen a mob of dingoes chase an emu into a fence, where it died of exhaustion. Sometimes, when Dad was camping out, he had to hang his food bag high up in a tree so the dingoes wouldn't tear it apart.

'Just you kids and your mother home, then?' asked Toothless.

'Yes. My little brother, Douglas, is three. And Price is twelve. He's out rabbiting today. Mr Akbar, the mailman, pays him for the skins. Price reckons he's head of the house when Dad's gone. But I don't.' She sighed. 'And we've got two sisters, Pearl and Esther, buried out the back. Mum says they weren't strong enough to grow big. Mum cries about my sisters sometimes. But I pretend not to notice. Mum says Pearl and Esther have gone to a better place. Price says she means heaven. I reckon she means Adelaide. It's got beaches with real water.' She paused to take a breath and her eyes slid again to the chaff bag. 'You've got a lot to carry. Is it heavy?'

'Used to it. Been on the road since I was thirteen.'

'That's about the biggest bag I've ever seen.'

Toothless slurped his tea like an animal that had found water in a drought. He spat a tea-leaf onto the ground.

Audrey copied by spitting a leaf of her own. Then she spat another through the gap where a tooth had fallen out. She liked the gap and hoped her new tooth wouldn't grow down too quickly. At home she would never be allowed to spit. Suddenly she felt more grown-up.

The breeze ruffled the trees and scattered dry leaves. Audrey looked down at the hot coals under the billy. Toothless had built a small sand wall around the camp fire so the wind couldn't blow coals and soot into the dry grass. Dad would like that. Toothless had been careful.

A sudden snap from the dense twiggy bushes behind Toothless made Audrey jump. Tea slopped from the pannikin onto her hand.

Toothless grunted. 'Caught something.'

Five

Toothless walked quietly for a large man. As though his feet didn't know the weight of his body. The bushes in this spot were the same height as the swagman and quite thick, so he vanished the moment he stepped through them. Audrey could tell which way he was heading by the cracking of twigs and rustle of leaves. Then the sound stopped.

Audrey's eyes were drawn to the chaff bag. Maybe she could take one little peek. The top of the bag was fastened with string and only loosely tied. It would be easy to undo.

She looked around, wishing she hadn't made Stumpy wait so far away from the camp. Audrey gave a low whistle that sounded like a bird call. If Stumpy heard it he would know she wanted him. That was their special signal. Stumpy was smart. He would tell her if it was all right to look in the bag. Silently, she urged him to hurry. Toothless could return at any moment.

Too impatient to wait for Stumpy, she put her pannikin down on the ground. Still seated with her legs crossed, she edged sideways, closer to the swagman's bag.

It wasn't stealing, because she wasn't going to take anything. She was only going to look.

The breeze freshened to tease the trees and bushes again.

Audrey froze. Was the swagman coming back?

But it was only Stumpy. He stood back, partly concealed by the bushes. She saw his eyes staring at her through a gap in the leaves.

Unsure what to do, she pointed to the swagman's mysterious bag.

Stumpy nodded. Audrey's heart beat faster. Nervously, she danced her fingers in the red sand, closer to the bag.

Then she stopped.

It didn't feel right. The bag belonged to Toothless.

Audrey erased her fingermarks in the sand with a sweep of her hand just as Toothless strode back into the clearing, growling under his breath.

Audrey jumped guiltily. Relief flooded through her at the same time. If she hadn't changed her mind about snooping, Toothless would have caught her with her hand in his bag.

The swagman sat down. He didn't seem to notice that Audrey had moved. 'Set some rabbit traps out back, but the spring's too light. Wind blew a twig into it and set it off.

Have to fix it later. Can't muck about with machinery when there's a lady visiting.'

Audrey was pleased to be called a lady, but also slightly embarrassed. She wasn't sure a lady would peek into other people's bags. But it didn't dampen her curiosity. 'Do you carry your own firewood?'

It might be a silly question, but she couldn't think of another. Soon she would have to ask straight out—or else forget all about the bag. But she wasn't sure she could forget. Whenever she tried to stop thinking about something, it always came back, bigger and louder, refusing to be ignored. Sometimes her thoughts shouted at her.

Toothless threw the dregs of his tea into a clump of spiky spinifex grass. 'Want to know what's in the bag, do you?'

Audrey shrugged as if she didn't really care.

Toothless sniffed. 'Heads.'

Six

Audrey gasped.

Toothless leaned over to drag the chaff bag closer. It rattled again.

He pulled the string at the top of the bag and the knot fell undone.

Perspiration broke out on Audrey's back.

Toothless reached inside the bag with his large sun-browned hand and pulled out a skull.

'I don't really have whole heads, mind you,' he said. 'Mostly jaws, with a skull or two.'

The skull was the wrong shape to be human.

Audrey relaxed. 'It's a sheep.'

'No flies on you, are there?' Toothless put the skull on the ground and dug around in his bag again. This time he pulled out a long jaw. The teeth were a funny shape, not like the teeth that Audrey had lost.

'Why do you carry sheep skulls around with you?'

Balancing the jawbone in his left palm, Toothless slipped his other hand into his back pocket. He pulled out a large pair of pliers, then fastened them onto a tooth. He wriggled the tooth back and forth.

Audrey's mouth dropped open. She only realised it when a bush fly got too close to her lips. Quickly, she clamped them shut again.

Cracking sounds came from the tooth. Then, with one last twist of the swagman's wrist and an even louder crack, the tooth popped out.

The swagman held it up, still pinched in the pliers. 'See?'

Audrey nodded. 'My tooth came out by itself.' She touched the gap with her fore-finger. 'When I was asleep.'

'I always wanted to be a dentist,' said Toothless, 'but never had much schooling. Not that good with the three Rs.'

'Three what?' asked Audrey.

'Reading, 'riting and 'rithmatic.' He flicked the sheep's tooth away, slipped the pliers into his pocket and replaced the sheep jaw in the bag. 'But I can be a bush dentist. All I need is a bit of practice, like. That's why they call me Toothless. Because I like pullin' teeth.'

'I know a swaggie called Bloke. She's a girl swaggie,' said Audrey. 'She's got no teeth. Not one. She sucks her meat off the bone. Bloke has lots of saliva that sort of melts her meat.'

'Too right?'

'Bloke gave *me* a nickname. Two-Bob, cos

she reckoned I'm crazy as a two-bob watch,' said Audrey. 'I do have two arms like a watch, and a round face. But I don't have numbers.'

They sat without speaking for a few minutes, busy with their own thoughts. A tiny skink darted across the sand and behind a rock.

Then Audrey said, 'I reckon you'd make a *good* dentist.'

Above his beard, the swagman's cheeks went red and shiny. 'It's a good thing to know who you are. What you want to be.'

'Maybe grown-ups ask children what they want to be because they're looking for ideas. Axshully ...' Audrey took a breath and tried again. 'Actually, *I've* got a really good idea.'

Seven

Audrey strode towards home. It didn't take long to put some distance between her and the swagman's camp. She wiped perspiration from her forehead with the back of her hand. 'Stumpy, I can't stop now.'

She kept walking, trying not to let him sidetrack her. 'I can *see* you behind that tree. I know hide-and-seek is your favourite game, but I've got things to do.'

Stumpy gave up and followed her, as he always did.

'Do you know why trees grow up and not sideways?' she asked.

Stumpy didn't answer.

'I don't know, either. But Toothless might. He's seen more trees than most people. I might ask him. Mum reckons I ask too many questions. She says some things don't have answers. But if there are questions, there has to be answers.'

Audrey waved her hand to frighten the flies away from her face. 'Should have brought my hat.' She knew there would also be flies on her back. But it was best not to disturb them or they would go for her face.

As she crossed the clearing around the house, she saw Price near the vegetable patch. He was squatting on his heels, stretching fresh rabbit skins over bent wires to dry them. A mob of flies hovered around him.

In the last few months, Price had grown taller in a hurry and his legs seemed too long for his body. But he was as skinny as ever. When he was younger, Dad called him 'Spindleshanks'. Price used to think it was funny, but not any more.

'He's caught lots of rabbits,' Audrey said to Stumpy. 'Now there won't be so many to munch Mum's cabbages.'

Rocks weighed down the wire fencing around the vegetable patch, but rabbits still sometimes burrowed underneath.

Once, when rabbits got into the vegetable patch, Audrey's mum had gone after them with a stick. It was the only time Audrey had heard her shout. It didn't worry the rabbits too much. They hopped off, then sent their cousins, aunties and uncles back to have a go at the rest of the vegetables.

Price looked up. He was hot and flushed. His sandy hair stuck out all over the place like a spinifex bush. His fingers were spotted with rabbits' blood.

Audrey screwed up her nose. The smell of fresh skins did strange things to her stomach.

She took a second look at her brother's messy hair. It was worse than usual. She put one hand to her mouth and whispered to Stumpy, 'Looks like he's been pulled through a bush backwards.'

'What was that?' asked Price.

'Nothing. I was talking to Stumpy.'

Her brother shook his head.

'You don't have to be so serious just because you're twelve.'

Price didn't argue. Instead he asked, 'Want a rabbit's foot for luck?'

'No, thanks.' Audrey couldn't understand how carrying a dead rabbit's foot could change your luck. It certainly didn't make things better for the rabbit.

Price shrugged and began stretching another skin.

'I found out what's in the swaggie's bag.' Audrey clasped her hands behind her back.

Her brother's eyes sparked with interest. 'What?'

'Skulls and jawbones.'

Price snorted. He sounded like a grumpy camel, except he didn't spit. 'Why do you always make things up?'

'Don't believe me, then.' Audrey held her head high as she marched past him. 'I'm going inside. I have something important to do. And it's a secret.'

'And can I have some rope?'

Eight

Audrey's mother stood at the kitchen bench with both hands plunged into a cut-down kerosene tin of water. She was soaking a kangaroo leg. Meat had to be salted to stop it going bad, but too much salt made it chewy and horrible to eat. Soaking the meat before cooking made it much tastier.

Kangaroo wasn't Audrey's favourite food. It was dark and strong-tasting.

'Toothless says thanks for the eggs and he's coming down later to do a job for you, Mum, and can I have a saucepan?'

said Audrey. Then she added, 'What's that noise?'

Mrs Barlow pushed the kangaroo leg deeper into the water. 'Douglas is being a kookaburra in the bedroom.'

'Oh. So can I have a saucepan, *please*?'

'Are you going to help me cook?'

Audrey shook her head. She wasn't ready to explain. Mum might cry. Imagining her mother in tears made Audrey's eyes sting with sympathy.

'Have you forgotten the chookyard?' Mrs Barlow reminded her gently.

'No. I haven't forgotten. I'll do it later. Promise. So can I have a saucepan?'

'Yes, but don't put dirt in it or dent it.'

'I won't.' Audrey went over to the fire-place. She thought hard for moment. If she chose the smaller saucepan that would leave the big ones for her family. She stood on tiptoe and grabbed a blackened pan from a hook, then plonked it on the wooden table. 'And can I have some rope?'

'How *much* rope?'

'I have to check something first, then I'll know.'

'I look forward to hearing your plans.'

Audrey dashed into the little bedroom she shared with Douglas. Price had a room of his own. It was an iron lean-to at the side of the house, hot in summer and cold in winter. But Price liked it because he didn't have to share, and he had a door that opened to the outside, not into the main house.

Douglas sat on the kangaroo-skin rugs with his elbows out. 'Kookookaakaa.'

Audrey gripped one end of her mattress and thin blanket and began rolling them up, along the bed frame.

Douglas jumped up and threw himself on the mattress, giggling.

'Hop off, Dougie. I can't do this if you're lying on it.'

'Pway a game.'

'You're a bird. Birds don't play games.'

He lay still, looking at her with a cheeky spark in his eyes. 'Kookookaakaa.'

She lifted the end she had rolled so far and tried to flick Douglas off. His giggles became a squeal. Then he leapt off the bed and ran around the room, flapping his arms.

Audrey found her mattress harder to roll up than she expected. And not just because of the interruption from the 'Douglas bird'. Mum had recently re-stuffed the mattress with fresh grasses so it was plump. As the grasses dried out, it would flatten. She glanced longingly at her chook-feather pillow. It would have to stay. She could only carry so much at once.

'Kookookaakaa,' said Douglas, even louder than before.

Audrey wrapped both arms around her mattress and blanket to carry them through the doorway. But the bedroll was too wide and she bounced backwards. Refusing to give up, she threw it over her left shoulder and carried it into the kitchen. She dumped the bedroll on the table, next to the saucepan, and hoped it wouldn't slip off.

Arms flapping, Douglas followed Audrey.

Mrs Barlow stared at Audrey but didn't ask questions. She dried her hands on her apron, then began selecting potatoes from the hessian bag in the corner.

Audrey returned to the bedroom, relieved that Douglas had stayed in the kitchen to flap around in there. She reached under her bed until her fingers touched metal and she pulled out a large tin decorated with a red and green parrot. Her cousin, Jimmy, had sent the tin from the city. It had been full of biscuits. Real biscuits. Ones he had bought in a shop, and they had all been the same size and shape. They'd been eaten a long time ago, but Audrey loved the tin almost as much as she had loved the crunchy sweet biscuits.

The tin was even more special now because it held treasure.

Nine

Audrey sat on the bare planks of her bed and opened the lid of the tin.

Price kept a collection of birds' eggshells on a length of string in his lean-to bedroom. Audrey collected her things in the tin.

Inside was a book called *Martin Rattler*. Jimmy had left it for her when he went back home to live with his dad in Adelaide. Cousin Jimmy had stayed with them for a year when his dad got into trouble. Audrey wasn't sure what sort of trouble. Her parents didn't talk about it. *Martin Rattler* was about a boy who had adventures at sea. Audrey couldn't picture water that stretched so far that no one could see the end of it.

There was also an eagle feather. She stroked it gently.

Then she unwrapped her green emu egg from its soft cloth. Dad once told her emus could foretell the weather. If there was going to be a drought they wouldn't lay eggs.

There were two pink quartz stones lying next to the emu egg. Audrey picked one up and turned it over, watching it glint.

Next, she scooped up her five sheep knucklebones, tossed them in the air and turned her hand over. Two knuckles landed on the back of her hand. The other three fell into the tin. She let the knucklebones she'd caught drop beside the others.

There was a tattered diary, another gift from her cousin Jimmy. It was maroon with the year 1930 written in black letters on the front. Every page up till the end of March was crammed with Audrey's large, uneven handwriting and drawings.

She couldn't leave the diary behind. There were so many of her private thoughts written in there. Things she didn't want to share—or forget. And what if Price saw she'd described him as having 'a head like a robber's dog'? That was after an argument, so she'd been cross with him. Although it was true—he often did look like a dog. Especially when he hadn't combed his hair. But usually he looked like a nice, friendly dog.

'Kookaakookaaa,' Douglas burst out.

Audrey jumped. Absorbed in her treasures, she hadn't noticed him sneaking in. He was on his hands and knees on the kangaroo-skin mat.

He flapped feebly, pretending he was still playing birds. But the look of curiosity on his face suggested he wanted to know what she was doing.

Audrey glared at him. 'What are you up to, Dougie?'

'Kooka hungwy,' said Douglas.

'Kookaburras eat worms and snakes.' Audrey replaced the lid on her treasure tin.

Douglas's arm-wings drooped.

'They whack them on the ground first,' said Audrey, 'to kill them.'

'I'm a boy now, not a kooka.'

Audrey carried her tin out to the kitchen and added it to the growing pile on the table. The square tin would be awkward to carry, but she couldn't leave it behind. 'Mum,' she said. 'I need the rope now.'

Her mother looked up from the potato she was peeling with a small knife. 'Now would be a good time to explain, dear.'

Audrey hesitated. Her idea had come so easily. Sorting through her things hadn't been so hard either. But telling her mother about her plan was going to be awkward.

'I'll visit sometimes so you won't miss me too much,' she began.

Douglas scampered into the kitchen. 'Want to eat boy food. I'm hungwy.'

Mrs Barlow ignored him. 'Audrey, why am I going to miss you?'

'I'm leaving, to be a swaggie.'

Ten

Mrs Barlow looked at the things on the kitchen table, then at Audrey.

Audrey's heart was beating hard.

'Well. If you've made up your mind, there's not a lot I can do,' said Mum. 'I wouldn't want to hold you back.'

Audrey's knees felt weak with relief. She hadn't wanted an argument just before leaving home.

'Want some tucker before you go?' her mum asked. 'And a cup of tea? It's no fun walking a long way on an empty stomach.

And then there's the weight you'll have to carry.'

Audrey nodded.

Douglas jiggled up and down on his bare feet. 'Hungwy.'

'How about you set the table and get out the jam, Audrey?' her mum said. 'I'll slice the bread and make a pot of tea.'

'Bwed,' said Douglas.

Suddenly Audrey realised it might be a long time before she saw her little brother again. She would miss the way Douglas flung himself at her legs and hung on, and the funny way he talked. And he was so adorable when he was asleep.

Mrs Barlow opened the back door and called out, 'Hungry, Price?'

Price yelled back that he wanted to finish stretching the rabbit skins.

Audrey picked up her mattress from the table and put it on the floor. Then she added the saucepan and tin of treasures. There wasn't room on the table for her swaggie's gear *and* morning tea.

Carefully, she placed three white teacups on their saucers, then added a clean teaspoon. She took three plates from a shelf and put them on the table. Audrey often set out the plates, but usually she paid no particular attention to it. Today was different. This could be the last time she did it. She noticed how smooth and cool the saucers were, the shape of the cup handles, and the clack as she sat them on the wooden table. The pot of jam was heavy and, when she removed the lid, she could smell sweet plums.

Mrs Barlow set down a plate of thickly-sliced bread and a pot of tea.

The moment she spread jam on Douglas's bread, he grabbed it and took a bite. He dropped it back on his plate and hopped down, jumped about, climbed back up on his chair for another bite, then ran back to the bedroom.

'He's having an emu's smoko. A drink

and a look around,' said Mrs Barlow. 'So, Audrey, where are you headed?'

Audrey didn't know exactly, but she didn't want to say so. 'Um ...' She waved her jam-smeared knife. 'That way.'

Mrs Barlow poured two cups of tea from a large teapot. 'What's that way?'

'Um ... things to find. Adventures.'

'Now that you're leaving,' said her mum, 'we might bring Price back into the house. He can have your bed.'

Audrey felt her chest tighten. She didn't want someone else sleeping on her bed, or storing their special things under it.

'What will you cook in the saucepan?'

Audrey wiped plum jam from her lip. 'Whatever I can find. Kangaroo, possum, maybe rabbit or a bird ...'

Although cockatoos were not such a good idea. Her dad had told her a story about a swagman who was so hungry he cooked a cockatoo. The swagman put a rock in the water with the cocky, then boiled it until the rock was soft. Only then was the cocky ready to eat.

'You'll need a trap and a sharp knife to catch rabbits,' said Mrs Barlow.

Audrey frowned. She hadn't thought about having to catch her food and kill it. At home, Mum, Dad or Price took care of that. 'Maybe I'll eat plants.'

'I could never work out which things are all right to eat in the bush. Quandongs are good for jam and tarts, of course. But things like paddymelons . . .' Mrs Barlow shook her head. 'If horses eat them, they can go blind.'

'Dad told me you watch what the birds eat.'

Mrs Barlow reached for a thick slice of bread. 'Yes, of course you can. But sometimes birds are able to eat things that upset human stomachs. If you're not sure, you can eat just a little of anything new, then wait to see if you become sick. If you do, then you know not to eat more.'

Audrey felt her enthusiasm for the swaggie's life begin to fade. But her things were already stacked along the wall. She had announced she was leaving. She couldn't back out now.

Eleven

When Audrey had a high fever, her mum had brought her broth to sip and laid cool damp cloths on her forehead. She'd fanned Audrey to make a cool breeze. Out in the bush, on her own, there would be no one to do those things for her.

'You're a brave girl.' Mrs Barlow spread jam on her bread, then sipped her tea. 'I'm sure you have a plan to protect yourself against dingoes and snakes. And then there are the mosquitoes. But you know how to rub your skin with animal fat or crushed ants' nest to stop the mozzies biting you. I'm sure you'll be fine. Too bad the mozzies are so awful at the moment.'

Audrey didn't like snakes. And she didn't fancy the idea of sharing her bedding with something that had fangs.

Mrs Barlow shook her head. 'I couldn't face being alone in the bush and having to cut a lump out of my own leg because a snake bit me.'

Audrey's stomach tightened. 'I won't be alone, exactly. Stumpy will come too.'

'Ah.'

Sometimes grown-ups said more with those sounds than they did with real words.

'Have you asked Stumpy if he *wants* to go?' asked her mum.

'He always goes where I go.' Audrey looked down at her half-eaten bread. She wasn't hungry any more.

'I'll pack you supplies,' said Mrs Barlow. 'When the bread goes hard, you can soak it in water.'

Many mornings, Audrey woke to the smell of freshly-baked bread. Her mum baked it in the outdoor oven Dad made from crushed ants' nest and wire netting. There would be no fresh bread in the bush.

And where would she find water? She knew to watch for the places where white cockatoos gathered at sunset. Her dad said cockatoos had to drink every day because they ate dry seeds. But it might take days to walk between billabongs. A long spell with no rain might dry up those billabongs, and *then* what would happen?

Only a little while ago, her idea of being a swaggie had been exciting. It meant not having to do chores like cleaning out the chookyard. It meant no brothers to annoy her, no one telling her what to do. She could spit whenever she felt like it. And she could lie under a starry sky figuring out important things like, Where does the wind start? Why don't dingoes bark? Is it better to be a sheep or a cow?

But now Audrey realised there were other things she hadn't thought about.

'You probably need a bit of time to get used to the idea,' she said. 'Mothers would, I reckon. I don't have to leave today. I could wait till tomorrow . . . or another day.'

'It's kind of you to think of me. Especially when you're ready to go.'

Audrey sat bolt upright. 'I know. I'll camp outside tonight, at the back of the house. You won't need to worry because you'll know I'm really close.'

'Good idea.'

'I have lots of good ideas.'

Mrs Barlow put down her cup of tea. 'I was afraid you'd say that.'

Twelve

Audrey held her breath against the smell of the chookyard. The bucket handle hurt her hand. Chooks didn't weigh much, but their manure did. Her mum was probably feeding them too much.

Struggling a little, but determined to manage, Audrey carried the bucket to the vegetable patch. The red sandy soil would grow vegetables as long as there was enough water. But sand didn't hold water very well. The stinky manure soaked up the water and held it for the vegetables.

She opened the gate and took the bucket over to Toothless. Her mum had asked him to weed. It was hot in the afternoon sun and he had cast aside his brown jacket. He knelt besides the neat rows and curled his whole hand around the weeds to drag them out.

He squinted as he looked up from beneath his broad hat-brim. 'You've got muscles in places other kids don't have places.'

Audrey tried not to look too pleased. She didn't want him to think she had tickets on herself.

She took off her own hat and fanned her face. 'We're flat out like lizards drinkin', aren't we?'

'Reckon so.'

Audrey knelt beside him and copied the way Toothless grabbed the weeds that grew between the carrots. There were lots of ways to pull weeds. Douglas tugged on anything that looked green, including the vegetables, and usually left half of the roots behind. So he was banned from weeding until he grew older. Mum pinched weeds out with her thumb and forefinger. Price ripped them out, flicking soil everywhere. Audrey used a little of each method, depending on her mood. Today, she felt like testing the swaggie's way. She curled her hand around the middle of a weed and pulled. It came away perfectly, roots and all.

'Mum always plants radishes with the carrot seeds,' said Audrey. 'The radishes break the ground so the soft little carrot leaves can come up.'

'That so?'

'And she washes the seeds in kerosene so they won't get eaten by birds or bugs.' Audrey dropped her weeds onto the pile between herself and Toothless. 'Price reckons it makes the carrots taste like kero. But I don't.'

Toothless grunted.

'Why are carrots orange?'

He shrugged. 'Maybe God ran out of other colours. Orange might have been the only one left.'

'Do you think people would eat carrots if they were brown?'

'Dunno.'

'Brown isn't as pretty as orange.'

Toothless scooped a handful of manure from the bucket and scattered it around the leafy carrot tops. Audrey guessed he had done this before. He knew not to put manure on top of the leaves or they would burn.

'If you were a carrot and you wanted to hide, it would be better to be brown,' said Audrey. 'Then people wouldn't see you and they wouldn't eat you.'

Toothless grinned.

''Course, carrots can't choose what colour they want to be, can they?'

'Guess not.'

'People can choose what they want to be,' said Audrey. 'I want to be a swaggie.

I might even meet up with my dad. Anyway, I'm going to sleep outside tonight.'

Toothless looked at her for a long moment before he answered. 'Sometimes people don't choose. Things choose people.'

'What do you mean?'

'I've been on the road most of my life. It's all I know. But sometimes . . .'

Audrey waited patiently. Toothless talked a bit like Dad. He would start a sentence, look around, have a think, then finish when he was ready.

'Sometimes I wish I had somewhere to belong, a family,' Toothless said finally.

Audrey thought about that. She had a family, but she was going away. Then she shrugged. She could come back and see them every year and tell them about her adventures.

'You must have seen some exciting places,' she said to Toothless.

'Too right. And in some places, if I could've fitted in, I would've stayed. Maybe.

I dunno. Most of my life I've been like a glove that didn't fit anybody's hand.'

Audrey pushed a tiny carrot back into the sandy soil. It had come up accidentally with the weeds. She hoped Toothless hadn't noticed.

'I've had some bad luck,' Toothless continued. 'If it was raining pea soup, I'd get hit on the head by the fork. And things are tough in the city now. There's more and more city blokes jumpin' the rattler. Freight trains are full of them. Can't get work in the cities.'

Toothless pushed back his battered hat and wiped sweat from his forehead with the back of his hand. 'At least, out here, I can always get a roo or a rabbit, and no one tells me to mind me p's and q's. But a family, now that would be something to make a bloke think twice about moving on. Fair dinkum.'

Audrey sat back on her heels.

'Aw. What am I saying?' said Toothless.

'I couldn't sleep on a regular bed any more. Can't stand a roof over my head. Got to have the open sky above me. And being on the road is better than a poke in the eye with a burnt stick, eh?'

'Can I ask you an important question?'

Toothless nodded.

'Does the sky touch the ground?'

'What's on the other side of the moon, do you think?'

Thirteen

Audrey lay outside on her swag. The kerosene lamps inside the house had gone out, one by one, and the sounds of her family preparing for bed had stopped. But the warm night was rich with noises.

'Stumpy, did you hear that?' Her voice was like a sigh with words.

Wind swept across the yard. The wood in the chook shed creaked like an old man with rickety joints. It took the slightest puff to make it creak. But so far, it hadn't fallen down. Then the hessian walls on the long-drop dunny fluttered. Audrey heard the goats bleating. They sounded like crying babies.

'Funny thing about wind, Stumpy,' Audrey whispered again. 'Sometimes you hear it rushing along, shaking trees, right beside you. But you can't feel it yourself. It's like a ghost wind.'

Then Audrey wished she hadn't said the word *ghost*.

It was comforting to hear her own voice, but if there was something scary out here in the dark, it might hear her and know where to find her. She wasn't sure what that 'something scary' would be. If it wasn't a ghost, it might be a bunyip. They lived near billabongs. Audrey's family didn't have a billabong nearby. But they did have a well. If a bunyip was thirsty, it might come to their well for water.

Price reckoned bunyips howled awfully. If you heard one, you'd never forget it. The hairs on your arms would stand up and your stomach would squirm. Audrey told herself that bunyips weren't real. But she couldn't help imagining fangs, fur, and sharp claws.

Something thumped nearby. *Boinng, boinng.*

She went rigid, not daring to move. Then she realised what it was and felt silly. 'Don't be scared, Stumpy. It's a roo. Big one by the sound of it. I hope it doesn't jump on me.'

A yellow moon was just rising. It was half in shadow, half brightly lit. Audrey liked trying to pick out the dark edge of the moon.

'What's on the other side of the moon, do you think?'

Audrey waited for Stumpy to answer. But he was unusually quiet.

Slipping her hands behind her head, Audrey stared up at the stars. They winked in different colours: bluish, red and white.

She began to wish she hadn't chosen to sleep outside. Douglas would be in their shared bedroom, sweaty and talking in his sleep. He might even be slobbering over his thumb. When he was asleep, his thumb sneaked into his mouth by itself. Price was in his lean-to, probably dreaming about moving into her room.

Her mum might have thought about her for a while, but now she'd be asleep. 'I wouldn't want Mum to cry too much when we leave home, not a big flood or anything,' Audrey confessed to Stumpy. 'But a few tears would be all right.'

Stumpy still did not answer. Was he already asleep, like everyone else?

Audrey felt as alone as a country dunny.

If she was a swaggie, like Toothless, every night would be like this. It might be weeks before she saw another person. Maybe months.

A dingo howled. The sound seemed to come from everywhere all at once.

Audrey sat up, her heart racing. She rolled sideways to get out from under her blanket, but her legs became tangled. She kicked the blanket away and scrambled to her feet. 'Wake up, Stumpy.'

She couldn't go back inside. Not till morning. Price might laugh at her. But she could do the next best thing—move closer.

Hurriedly, she rolled her mattress and blanket into an untidy bundle. Her own breathing, loud and fast, was making her even more nervous. Audrey was glad she had left her billy, saucepan and treasure tin inside for tonight. It made her swag lighter.

Audrey headed for the house. Her right foot caught on something and she almost tripped. The end of the blanket was dragging. She flicked it to one side, letting it dangle in the dust beside her. The half-moon helped her walk the rest of the way without tripping.

Audrey dropped her mattress close to the back of the house, then smoothed it out as best she could. Her mum was sleeping on the other side of the wall. Knowing she was close made Audrey feel a lot safer.

'Move back, Stumpy,' she whispered, 'You're crowding me.'

She wriggled down between the blanket and the grass-filled mattress.

'What did you say?' Audrey listened to Stumpy for a moment, then nodded. 'You're right. Mum needs me to help her. Especially because her leg's bad. When the flying doctor stuck her back together, I think he got some parts the wrong way round. I've changed my mind about being a swaggie. I'd better stay home.'

She swiped at a mosquito near her face. Although she couldn't see it, its whine was loud. As soon as she fell asleep it would dive and bite.

'If I can't be a swaggie, I know something else I can be,' said Audrey. 'I'm not telling you what it is yet. It's a surprise.'

Fourteen

Mrs Barlow lowered the forked branch that held the clothes line high above the ground. Although the line was secured at each end to wooden posts, the forked branch stopped it sagging in the middle. She unpegged a sheet and dropped it into the basket.

Audrey opened the kitchen door.

'Mum! Have you got any string to tie these up?' She clutched at the loose waistband of the trousers she was wearing.

'What happened to your dress?'

'Price said I could have these. They're too small for him.'

'Pwice,' said Douglas. He sat on the ground, legs crossed, scraping at the sandy soil with a sturdy stick. Sand sprayed sideways, peppering Audrey's feet.

'What are you doing, Dougie?'

'Digging a hole to wet the wabbits out.'

Audrey giggled.

Douglas looked surprised, as though he couldn't see anything funny in what he was doing. Which made Audrey giggle again. Watching her little brother, and listening to his funny talk, reminded her how happy she was to be home and not on the road. If she'd left to be a swaggie, she would have missed Douglas.

Toothless had left the previous afternoon after the chores were done. She imagined him on a dusty road, carrying his big chaff bag full of jaws, and whistling.

'There's a spare pair of braces in the big chest in my room,' said Mrs Barlow.

Audrey dashed back inside.

Her mum's dark wooden chest was at the foot of the double bed. Audrey knelt and lifted the lid, grunting with effort. The smell of wild rosemary floated out.

The chest was full of clothes. On top was a rolled-up cloth that looked like an old nappy. Something was inside it. Curious, Audrey unwrapped it and found a familiar dented sardine tin. She and Price had used it as an engine when they played trains. Price didn't play trains any more. He said he was too old for games. Audrey rewrapped the sardine-tin train and put it aside.

Then she took out a neatly-folded knitted baby's jacket. It was tiny and smelt like soap. Audrey ran her fingers over the soft wool. She wasn't sure which of her sisters had worn the jacket. Neither of them had grown very big. Esther died when she was three days old. Pearl managed to hang on for two years, but she had been sick for most of that time.

Audrey wondered what it would have been like if Pearl or Esther had been stronger. She would've had sisters to play with, to share secrets and biscuits. Though maybe not share the biscuits.

Gently, Audrey refolded the baby's jacket and smoothed it down.

Her mum's wooden chest was like Audrey's own treasure tin under her bed. It was private. Audrey didn't want to look any more.

The braces were at the top, to the right. She picked them up and closed the lid.

Fastening the two front clips of the braces to her trousers was easy, but Audrey couldn't quite manage the back.

Clutching the wide waistband with one hand, she headed outside again.

Half-closing her eyes against the sun, the way her dad did, Audrey loped towards her mum at the clothes line. She swayed from one foot to the other. 'I can't reach the back of these braces.'

'Turn around.' Mrs Barlow's fingers fiddled with the clips.

The trousers were so big, Audrey could hide breakfast, lunch and tea inside the waistband. But at least they would now stay up.

'What are you up to, Audrey?'

She turned to face her mum. 'Why do you think I'm up to something?'

'You're always up to something.' Mrs Barlow bent forward to look Audrey in the eyes. 'Apart from the sudden appearance of your brother's cast-off trousers, there's that funny walk.'

'Dad walks like that.'

'That's because your father spends much of his life on the back of a camel.'

Audrey nodded. 'I might have to do that too.'

'But don't you think camels are cranky and smell funny?'

'Not all camels. Just Dad's. The one called Dribble snots on people.'

As Audrey took a breath to continue, a fly whipped into her mouth and stuck in her throat. She coughed, once, twice, then gagged. Turning aside, she tried to suck the fly back up so she could spit it out. Her stomach heaved. Finally, she hoiked the soggy fly out and onto the ground.

'Pah. Pah.'

Although the fly was now drowning in saliva on the sandy soil, Audrey could still feel where it had tickled her tonsils.

'Are you all right?' Mrs Barlow patted Audrey's back.

'*Blasted* fly,' said Audrey.

Her mum's hand went still. 'I *beg* your pardon?'

'Dad says blasted.'

'You're not Dad. You're a little girl. Words like that are not nice coming from a girl's mouth.'

'I know other words,' said Audrey. 'And they're much worserer than b . . .' She saw the look on her mum's face and stopped.

'Much worserer than that one.'

'It's worse, not worserer.'

'Sure is.' Audrey wiped her mouth with the back of her hand, the way she'd seen Toothless do it. 'Fair dinkum worse.'

'Audrey Barlow, I'd say *spit it out*,' said her mum, with a twinkle in her eyes. 'But it appears you just did that. What's going on?'

'I started thinking. Actually, I don't stop really, except when I'm asleep. Then I dream. Which is a kind of thinking, except I can't make my thoughts go where I want. But sometimes when I'm asleep, I can make my dreams go where I want. But that's really half-dreaming and half-thinking, so it doesn't count.'

'Dweams,' said Douglas, as he continued to dig holes with a stick.

'Is that your answer, Audrey?' asked Mrs Barlow. 'It sounded more like a question.'

'I'll give you an example.'

'Where did you learn that big word?'

Mrs Barlow flicked out a pair of Price's

trousers, then folded them in half, before placing them in the basket.

'From the dictionary in the lounge room.' Audrey smiled. 'It's got lots of good words in it.'

'I bet.'

'It's like this . . .' Audrey stroked her mum's arm, to help her understand. 'Remember when I was four and I used to pick my nose? Dad told me that my finger was getting too big and it would get stuck up there. Well, now I'm older, so I've stopped.'

'I'm so glad.'

'I'm doing another change. The swagman idea didn't work out, so I've thought of something else. I'm sick of being a girl. We don't get enough words. I'm going to be a man.'

Fifteen

Audrey stood by her bedroom window and peered into the hand-mirror she'd borrowed from her mother. She tilted back her head, then turned it from side to side.

'You coming, or what?' Price's voice surprised her from the doorway.

Audrey jumped.

'What are you doing?' he asked. 'Staring at yourself in the mirror?'

'No.'

'Yes, you were. I just saw you.'

Audrey slapped the mirror down on her mattress. 'I was checking something.'

'What?'

'I was looking to see if I had nose hairs.'

'Nose hairs?'

'Don't copy everything I say.' Audrey flounced past him. 'Yesterday I decided to be a man. And men have hairs sticking out of their noses. Dad does. I've seen Mum trimming them with scissors. She nicked his nose once and made it bleed.'

Price followed Audrey through the tiny lounge room to the kitchen. 'You can't be a *man*,' he said.

'Toothless reckons people can be anything they want. They just have to make up their minds to it,' she said. 'That's why he's got jaws in his bag. I made up my mind to be a man.'

She swung into her rolling lope, the way she imagined her dad and other men, like Toothless, walked. Each of her trouser legs was tucked up to make a fat cuff. Then she plucked at her braces, making them snap against her chest. She lowered her voice to make it as deep as she could. 'Fair dinkum, Price. Let's get this job done.'

'You're as mad as a cut snake,' said Price.

'No, I'm ...' For a second, Audrey had reverted to her usual voice. Then she remembered and lowered it again. 'Reckon I should give you a hand.'

'Reckon *not*.' Price grabbed a square tin of kerosene. 'You'd get in the way. You can watch.'

Audrey pouted.

'Even if you were a man, which you're *not*, I'm the oldest.'

'Fair enough, mate.' Audrey followed her brother outside.

She was tempted to give her bird-whistle, the signal that she wanted Stumpy. But she held back. She'd told him that she had man-things to do today and couldn't play children's games. He had to stay out bush till she called him back.

Audrey strode behind Price, carefully avoiding the patch of three-cornered jacks. Although the prickles were tiny, they were hard, with sharp points. And it was difficult picking them out of the soles of her only pair of boots.

Yesterday's wind had blown itself out. The hessian walls on the long-drop dunny hung straight and still.

'Eggs,' shouted Douglas, from inside the chookyard. He was helping Mum.

The chooks were letting them go again. Maybe their stomachs had finally got too big.

'Price, how many eggs can a chook carry in its stomach at the same time?' she asked.

Her brother shrugged.

When they reached the long-drop, Price screwed up his nose. 'This dunny's ripe.'

Usually a dose of lime got rid of the smell. But not this time.

Audrey tugged the trousers to loosen the knees so she could sit back on her heels. 'Dad reckons you don't have to empty your own dunny in the city. A bloke comes round at night, like a ghost, when you can't see him. He's got a cart they call a honey cart. If you're rich, you can have a real flush, with water. They must have lots of water in the city if they can pour it down dunnies.'

Price unscrewed the lid of the kerosene tin. Now there was also the smell of kerosene in the air.

'If you want to be a man, you'll have to do jobs like this one,' said Price.

With a firm shake of her head, Audrey said, 'If I'm a man, I can say no. I'll tell someone else to do it.'

'Who?'

'You.'

'You're a ning-nong.' Price lifted the tin and splashed kero into the dark hole.

'Dad doesn't put that much in,' said Audrey.

Price shook more kerosene into the hole.

'You'd better stop now.'

'I know what I'm doing,' said Price.

'Do men always know what they're doing?'

Price shrugged.

'Then why do you always say it?' Audrey slowly scratched at her cheeks as though she had a beard growing there. Dad and Toothless did that. She wasn't sure whether their beards were itchy or if they just liked scratching. There were lots of man-things she hadn't yet worked out.

Price gave another generous shake of the tin, replaced the lid and put it outside the dunny.

'Be careful,' said Audrey.

'I know what I'm ...' Price cleared his throat. 'It'll be okay. Move back if you're worried.'

Audrey obeyed.

Price took a matchbox from his pocket, lit a match and threw it into the open hole.

There was an enormous *whoomph*, followed by a bang. A rush of heat knocked Audrey backwards.

Sixteen

Hot, kerosene-soaked fumes filled Audrey's throat. There was loud crackling and hissing.

'Audrey ... Price!' Their mum's anxious voice calling from the chookyard sounded like a distant echo.

Audrey blinked. There seemed to be a lot of blue. Her head was fuzzy, as though she wasn't properly awake. Then the fuzziness cleared. She realised she was lying on her back. The blue was the sky.

She looked over at Price. He, too, was on his back.

The hessian dunny walls were ablaze. Bluish flames leapt into the air.

Audrey's stomach squeezed into a knot. 'You're not dead, are you, Price?'

He sat up. 'I don't think so.'

'Lucky Stumpy is out bush for a while. He doesn't like fire.'

Mrs Barlow limped towards them, her face tight with worry. 'Are you two all right?' She sounded breathless.

Dougie bounced along behind her as though his feet were on springs.

'Yes,' answered Audrey. 'We're all right.'

She and Price had just meant to clean out the dunny hole with fire. They had almost cleaned *themselves* up with it. And now there was no hole at all. The sandy soil had collapsed in the explosion.

Red-faced, Mrs Barlow flopped beside Audrey and grabbed her hand.

Audrey felt her mother trembling.

Douglas leapt up and down. 'Pwetty fire.'

'Lucky we cleared a good patch around

the house,' said Mrs Barlow at last.

Price crawled across to sit beside his mother. He patted her shoulder. 'Sorry, Mum. But you've been wanting proper walls and a door for a long time. Now you can have them.'

His eyebrows and the front of his hair looked odd.

'You've singed your hair,' said Mrs Barlow.

Price put his hand to his fringe and bits fell off.

'Lucky he's a man,' said Audrey. 'He knew what he was doing.'

'Birds don't read or write and they get on all right.'

Seventeen

Mrs Barlow gently eased Douglas away from the kitchen meat safe. 'Leave that, Dougie. It's lesson time now.'

Hessian sat in a shallow tray of water at the top of the safe. The wet hessian draped down each side of a wooden frame and helped keep the meat cool, especially when a breeze blew through it. The hessian also kept flies out. And to stop ants getting in, each of the meat safe's four legs stood in a tin of water.

Douglas flicked his wet hands. Damp

spots appeared on the hard mud floor.

Audrey crossed one knee over the other, then smoothed down her yellow dress. It was the only one of her three dresses that had no patches on it. She thumped her elbows on the kitchen table and pushed the pencil and paper away.

'What's the matter, Audrey?' Mrs Barlow removed her apron and hung it behind the door.

'I don't like lessons.'

'You must learn to read and write properly.'

Audrey sighed noisily. 'Birds don't read or write and they get on all right.'

'But all they do is fly around and look for things to eat. You'd soon be bored with that.'

From where Audrey was sitting, the kitchen window was a square of blue sky. A black crow flew across it. Its *caa, caa, caa* cry made Audrey feel even more restless. She imagined skimming on a warm updraft of air. Everything on the ground would look small. Even the people. The crow was free to fly wherever it wanted. It didn't have to do chores like emptying chookyards or fixing dunny holes. Nor did it have to do lessons.

Somewhere outside, Toothless was walking the track, feeling the wind on his face. He would be clutching his chaff bag full of sheep jaws, dreaming about yanking their teeth.

Also out there, swaying on the back of a dusty camel, would be her dad. Audrey pictured him with his hat brim low, shading his eyes from the sun. His pipe would be in his mouth. Not lit. He didn't smoke any more, but he couldn't give up the pipe. He liked the feel of it. A bit like little Douglas when he was teething. He had chewed on a stick and wouldn't let anyone take it from him.

Stumpy was just outside the kitchen, humming. Audrey could hear him, but she didn't know the tune. He wanted her to know he was there. He made noises some-times, humming or coughing to get her attention. But she couldn't play until lessons were over.

'I don't want to be a girl learning to write,' she protested. 'Fair dinkum.'

When they were younger, she and Price sometimes ran and hid in the scrub at lesson time. But they didn't do that any more. It wasn't fair to run away from a mother who had a gammy leg.

'What do you want to be then, Audrey?' asked Mrs Barlow.

Frowning, Audrey thought hard. The swagman idea hadn't worked. Swaggies had to hunt their own food, find water and look after themselves when they were sick. At night, a swaggie had to lie in the dark, listening to all the other creatures who shared the bush. Knowing that some of them bit or chewed.

Being a man wasn't too good either. They blew up dunnies and singed their hair. Sure, they used words that girls were not allowed to say. But a man always had to know what he was doing. Or, at least, he had to pretend that he did. Men didn't get to play games like hide-and-seek or have cubbyhouses and pretend pirate ships.

Suddenly she had a new idea.

Eighteen

Audrey looked down at the paper and pencil on the table. 'I don't want to be the girl having lessons. I want to be the teacher. Can I, Mum? Can I be the teacher? It's easy. All you have to do is tell people what to do.'

'Is that so?' Her mum raised one eyebrow. 'All right, Audrey. You might find out how hard it is for me to get you and Price to sit still.'

She limped to the kitchen door and opened it. 'Price,' she called. 'Now, please!'

Price yelled something. His words were muffled.

'Be quick,' said Mrs Barlow. 'Gentlemen to the left of the house, remember. Ladies to the right.'

Audrey giggled. Since the dunny blew up, the family had to kick the bushes instead. It was a bit of a nuisance tramping out to the bushes several times a day for privacy. But Audrey didn't mind too much. Not everyone got to explode a dunny. Audrey had already written it all down in a letter to her cousin, Jimmy, in Adelaide. He'd be so jealous.

'Quick. Quick,' said Douglas.

'Can Stumpy come in for lessons too?' Audrey asked her mum.

'I don't think so, Audrey. There aren't enough chairs.'

Audrey's shoulders slumped. Then she pushed back her chair. 'I'll be back in a minute.'

She dashed through the lounge room into

her bedroom and reached up to the clothing hook on the wall.

The kitchen door squeaked open. Then Audrey heard her mum ask Price if he had washed his hands.

Price mumbled and there was a thump. Audrey guessed that was her brother throwing himself into his chair.

Audrey dragged her mother's old green dress over her head. The colour suited her, but it was far too long and dragged on the ground. It was her one dress-up outfit. When Mum was finished with her clothes, she usually cut them down to make smaller clothes for Audrey or her brothers. But Mum let her keep the green dress.

It was faded and ripped at the back. The material was so thin you could spit through it. But it still had all of its red buttons in a line down the front, and only three of them were broken.

Audrey used to have an old hat of her mum's too. But one day the wind had snatched it from her head and tossed it into the goat pen. Sassafras ate it.

Now for her bead necklace. It was all colours of the rainbow, with only a few beads missing. Audrey looped it around her neck three times. Then she tied her two thick plaits together at the back with a piece of string.

Breathless from hurrying, she held up the hem of the green dress and stumbled back into the kitchen.

From the corner of her eye she saw Stumpy peering in through the kitchen window. She refused to look directly at him. If she did, he might make her laugh.

Price screwed up his face. He looked like a dried plum. 'It's lessons, Audrey. Not playtime.'

'I'm not playing. I'm the teacher,' said Audrey. 'You have to call me Miss Barlow.'

Her brother threw a questioning look at their mother.

Mrs Barlow nodded. 'Yes, it's true. I have

some mending to do, in the lounge room.'

'But . . .' Price began.

'Just for today.'

Douglas scrambled onto the chair next to Price. 'Pway teachers too.'

Audrey stood as tall as she could. 'There's only one teacher. Me. But you can be a boy learning to read.'

Douglas giggled.

Price glared at Audrey.

She tried to think of something to say. 'Today we are doing alphabet letters.'

'The alphabet *is* letters,' grumbled Price.

'That's what I said.' Audrey sniffed. 'And you have to call me Miss Barlow.'

'I will not,' he said. 'I don't call Mum, *Miss Mum*, do I?'

'She doesn't want to be called *Miss*. I do.'

Price glared even harder.

'I changed my mind,' said Audrey. 'Let's do something different. Not the alphabet. Let's do questions.'

'Questions?' said Price.

'Qwestons.' Douglas stuck his thumb firmly in his mouth.

'I do the questions. You do answers. Ready?' Clasping her hands behind her back, Audrey tried to look clever. She pushed her mouth into a pout and half-closed her eyes. 'I want you to vestigate this—when you have a bath, why doesn't the water get inside your skin?'

'The word is *in*vestigate,' said Price. 'Not vestigate.'

'It's *in*vestigate if you look *in* something, like a book. But we only have four books and they don't say things about baths. It's vestigate if you don't look in something, but you think about it.'

Price tapped his pencil on the table. 'I don't want to think about it. It's a silly question.'

'No, it's not . . .' Audrey aimed a stare at Douglas. 'Young man, don't suck your thumb.'

Douglas looked behind him, searching for the person called 'young man'.

'You, Dougie. You can't suck your thumb.'

Douglas's face went red. He sniffed loudly. The sniffs turned into whimpering. His thumb stayed in his mouth.

Audrey hitched up her skirt and hurried to put her arm around Douglas's shoulders before Mum came in to stop the lessons. 'You can suck your thumb if you want. Don't cry.'

His whimpering faded, but he kept sucking his thumb.

Mum's voice came from the next room. 'Dougie's a bit young for school, Miss Barlow. Why don't you send him in here?'

Douglas didn't wait for Audrey to give permission. He shot her a sulky look, slid off the chair, and took his thumb into the lounge room.

Teaching was not as much fun as Audrey had expected. Douglas was too little. Price argued with everything she said. Being the teacher had seemed a good idea at first. But learning to read and write was a lot easier than trying to make other people do it.

'My pencil broke.' Price held it up. 'I can't write anything.'

'I quit!' Audrey put both hands on her hips. 'You can grow up to be a iggorant bird, looking for food.'

'The big one will be the dad.'

Nineteen

Audrey stepped out of her cubbyhouse. Although she had three of them, she'd chosen this one because its thick brush roof gave more shelter from the sun. The walls were also made of brush, but there was no door, just an opening. She didn't know how to make a door, but that didn't matter. This way, the wind could blow through more freely.

There was a crackling sound, as if someone had stepped on dry grass. She stared through the scrub.

'Did you hear something, Stumpy?'

It was probably just birds or a kangaroo.

The quandong stones hanging on strings from her hat jiggled back and forth. Flies still hovered around her face, but not as many. They were frightened off by the swinging stones. There was a gap where a stone was missing. Audrey hoped Price would give her one to replace it. He had a bag of them that he used for marbles. Price wasn't too old to play marbles.

Audrey's stomach rumbled. 'It's too hot to play pirates or flying doctors. And I'm hungry.'

Stumpy agreed.

'Let's go home.'

Most of the grasses were withering in the hot sun. But there was plenty of grey saltbush. Scraggy, with twiggy branches, the tallest of the bushes were only as high as Audrey's waist.

'Saltbush can last for a year without water,' Audrey told Stumpy as they skirted the bushes. 'Fair dinkum, a year is a long time. Almost forever.'

A skink shot across the red sand, just missing her feet. Audrey jumped. She wasn't scared of them, but they dashed out so quickly.

She stopped walking and pointed. 'Look, there *was* something moving.'

Ahead of her, through the trees, she saw an emu with a line of striped chicks behind him as though they were playing follow-the-leader. The chicks seemed to appear and disappear between the saltbush. Audrey hoped the grown-up emu wouldn't lose any of them.

'The big one will be the dad. Emu dads look after the babies.' Audrey felt sad. 'I wish *our* dad would come home.' His latest trip out bush had been a long one. She couldn't remember exactly how long. But it seemed like forever. 'Do you think a year and a long time and forever are the same?'

Stumpy didn't have a clue.

Warm red sand slipped between Audrey's sandals and the soles of her feet as she headed home. 'Lucky tomorrow's Saturday, Stumpy. I reckon I need a bath.'

On days when the wind was strong, sand flew into the house and got into everything. Audrey understood why her mum wanted real glass windows instead of hessian. But Audrey was pretty sure the sand would still find a way into the house.

As she neared the track that led home, a flock of cockatoos suddenly rose into the air, squawking and complaining.

She squinted against the bright sunlight. 'Someone's coming.' Audrey began to run. 'Dad!'

Twenty

Red sand puffed around Audrey's feet as she ran. The quandong stones swung wildy, bobbing against her face.

'Try to keep up, Stumpy,' she panted.

She kept an eye on the ground because she didn't want to put her foot down a rabbit hole or tread on a snake. The scrub thinned as it met the track. Someone was coming towards them on a camel. Audrey put one hand up to shield her eyes from the glare. A water mirage shimmered along the sand.

'But Dad took both camels with him, and where's Grease?' said Audrey. 'He and that old dog are always together. Just like you and me, Stumpy.'

Then Audrey realised the shape of the rider was wrong for Dad. Either he had an enormous head or he was wearing a turban.

Audrey slowed down, her chest tight with disappointment. Her feet felt strangely heavy. She had hoped so hard that it was Dad. Her face flamed with heat.

But any visitor was better than none. Especially this visitor. He brought letters and news.

The man on the camel wore a white turban and a long-sleeved shirt over loose trousers. His skin was brown and he had a long, hooked nose. He held a book in his hands, which he was reading as he rode.

'Mr Akbar!' Audrey waved at him.

Mr Akbar looked up from his book and raised a hand in greeting. As he drew closer he smiled down at Audrey.

'*Salaam aleikum,*' said Audrey. She wished him 'peace', just as he'd taught her on earlier visits. In Mr Akbar's country that was how they said 'hello'.

Mr Akbar's smile broadened as he wished Audrey peace in return.

'Where are your other camels?' asked Audrey.

Mr Akbar owned seven camels. Although he didn't bring them all, he often had a string of two or three with him.

'Ah ... trucks.' He sniffed and tucked his book into a saddle bag.

Skipping alongside Mr Akbar on his camel, Audrey wondered if a truck had run over his other camels. She'd seen a truck once, but it wasn't big enough to squash six camels at the same time.

'I released my other camels into the bush,' said Mr Akbar. 'They are no longer needed. Perhaps, this is my last visit. A truck will bring your mail from now on.'

Audrey wasn't sure whether to say she

would miss Mr Akbar or that it would be exciting to see the truck. So she said nothing. Privately she thought she would never give Stumpy away. Not even in exchange for a truck.

'Peanuts!' Mr Akbar exclaimed.

Audrey tried not to laugh, but ended up snorting. When Mr Akbar was annoyed, he said 'peanuts' as though it was a swearword. He had better words than that. But Mum had warned Audrey not to remember them. When Mr Akbar got really fired up, he rolled his eyes and spittle shot from his mouth. He didn't spit on purpose. He just forgot to swallow.

The ropes binding Mr Akbar's belongings creaked and the water in his canteen swished as his camel swayed along the path. Its feet drummed on the sand.

Audrey couldn't wait any longer. She crossed her fingers for luck and asked, 'Have you got a letter for me?'

Twenty-one

Audrey, Mr Akbar, Price and Mrs Barlow sat outside the kitchen door on kerosene tins. Douglas waddled back and forth to the chookyard. His hands were tucked under his armpits, which made his elbows stand out like wings. Today he was a chook.

Flies clung to the back of the house where it was shady. They always found the coolest wall.

Price's smile stretched from his left ear to his right as he jingled Mr Akbar's coins in the pocket of his shorts. Price had worked hard, snaring rabbits and stretching the skins. And Mr Akbar had paid a fair price.

Audrey wondered if Price was rich now, then decided he probably wasn't. Rich people didn't live in houses with mud floors and no glass in the windows.

Mr Akbar had brought letters. Audrey's was tucked under her pillow. She longed to rip open the neat envelope and read the words that had been written just for her. But it was good manners to give Mr Akbar something to eat first, and chat with him. He had travelled a long way since they'd last seen him—which had also meant months without letters.

'Another scone, Mr Akbar?' Mrs Barlow offered him the plate.

He had picked the right day to call. Maybe he had a good nose for the aroma of scones.

Mr Akbar shook his head. 'No, no, no. As God is my witness, I am full to bursting.'

Smiling, Mrs Barlow insisted.

They all knew that Mr Akbar always said no at least twice, and then dived in. Audrey counted to ten before he finally agreed.

'It would be impolite of me not to eat more. You have gone to much trouble, Mrs B.'

Audrey's dad had called Mum 'Mrs B' for so long, that other people did too. Her real name was Everhilda, but that was a mouthful. Audrey stuck to 'Mum'.

Mr Akbar took one scone, then a second. And a third. 'To save you having to offer me the plate yet again,' he said.

'And how have you been, Mr Akbar?' Mrs Barlow sipped her tea while she waited for him to empty his mouth.

It took a while. He didn't seem to understand that scones were supposed to be eaten a bite at a time. With him, it was all or nothing.

'I am well, thanks God.' He nodded. 'Although, only some little time ago I almost died.'

Price and Audrey exchanged a look. If everything Mr Akbar said was true, then he'd had more adventures than you could shake a stick at. More than all the other men in Australia put together.

'I made camp two days south,' he said, 'and woke in the night to a tickle on my face.'

He paused, waiting for them all to think about the horrors that lurked in the dark.

Audrey shivered, remembering the night she slept outside. Even Stumpy had been nervous.

Mr Akbar burped loudly. A morsel of scone flew from his mouth. Burping was a sign of enjoying food in the country where Mr Akbar grew up. Audrey imagined a large family, all burping at the same time. Instead of playing cards at night, they could have burp competitions.

'I kept my body still, but carefully reached out to strike a match,' continued Mr Akbar. 'Then I saw what was tickling.'

Price sneaked a hand out towards the scone plate. He had eaten nearly as many as Mr Akbar. Audrey had lost count of the exact number, but it was a lot. She took another one herself, before they were all gone.

Douglas ran back from the chookyard to weave in and out between them.

Mr Akbar's eyes popped wide open. 'It was a death adder.'

'Def!' repeated Douglas.

'If I had moved,' explained Mr Akbar, 'I would be in heaven before my time.'

'But with a sore face,' said Audrey. 'Even if you wanted to go to heaven, it wouldn't be worth getting bitten on the face by an adder.'

Mr Akbar leaned forward and stared fiercely at each of them in turn. 'Death adders are devious.'

'What's deevis?' asked Audrey.

'Adders *trick*,' he said. 'They disguise their bodies in grasses and cross their tails in front of the mouth. If a small animal comes close, the adder wriggles its tail. The animal grabs at the tail. Suddenly the adder *strikes* with his fangs.'

Douglas squealed.

Audrey winced. 'Our dog, Lightning, got bitten by a snake and he died.'

'Peanuts,' said Mr Akbar.

Mrs Barlow handed her cup of tea to Audrey and lifted Douglas onto her lap. He stuck his thumb in his mouth.

'Snakes are deevis, all right,' said Audrey. 'Mr Akbar, do you reckon dogs go to heaven? How come we don't see their legs hanging down?'

Twenty-two

'Mr Akbar, have you found a wife yet?' asked Mrs Barlow.

For as long as Audrey could remember, Mr Akbar had talked of his search for a wife. One time there actually was a woman that he liked, but on his next visit he had called her a 'peanut'. So Audrey guessed it hadn't worked out too well.

'I am an intelligent man, clean, with a quick brain, yet I cannot find a wife.'

'Maybe wives don't like the smell of camels,' said Audrey. She wanted to mention the spitting, too, but a warning glance from her mum suggested it was better not to say more.

Mr Akbar flicked scone crumbs from his long, thin beard. 'Where is your husband, Mrs B?'

Mrs Barlow let Douglas wriggle off her lap. 'Somewhere near Parachilna, I think.'

Mr Akbar said nothing. He began stroking his beard the way people petted their dogs.

The silence stretched.

Mr Akbar's face had gone very still, and so had his tongue.

Audrey's chest tightened. Was something wrong?

'What is it, Mr Akbar?' Although Mrs Barlow spoke gently, her face showed worry lines.

They all stared, waiting for him to say what was on his mind.

He looked towards the low hills on the horizon as though they held a secret that only he could see. Then he seemed to shake himself back to the present. 'Oh, I am so humbly sorry that I forget. I have something for the young lady.' He nodded to Audrey. 'A gift.'

Audrey suspected he was changing the subject on purpose. But even so, a flash of excitement shot through her. 'You've got a present, for me?'

Mr Akbar reached into a deep pocket in his baggy trousers and pulled out something wrapped in cloth. He rose and stepped towards Audrey. With both hands, he offered the gift.

'I met a man on the road who asked me if I was travelling this way. I said, "Yes", so he said, "There is a young lady with eyes green like winter grass, you must give this to her, to remember me by".'

Audrey unwrapped the cloth. Inside was a sheep jawbone. It had a row of teeth, with one missing, right in the middle.

She grinned. 'You met Toothless.'

'Yes, I remember his name had something to do with faces. This man, he makes tea that tastes like tar.'

'That's him, all right.'

Audrey leaned forward to show her older brother the jawbone. 'See Price? I told you the swaggie had skulls and jaws in his bag.'

'Mr Akbar.' Mum's voice cut sharply through their chatter. 'Tell me about my husband.'

'I have not seen your husband.' He waved a hand towards the sky. 'It is only ... I heard news of a fire near Parachilna. My friend, Jamal, had to run for his life. There was not much time to let his camels go loose. It was a big fire. Much smoke and flames.'

The colour drained from Mum's face, leaving it whiter than flour. 'I am sorry to hear about the fire, Mr Akbar. But I am sure my husband will be fine. He's a strong and clever man. He's lived in the bush all his life. And, by now, he should be well on his way home. I expect him any day.'

Mr Akbar nodded. 'Of course. Your husband will be safe.'

But the look in his eyes told Audrey that Mr Akbar was not sure about his own words.

'That man flew from London on a moth.'

Twenty-three

The kerosene lantern spluttered. Shadow shapes leaped up the lounge room walls as the flame flickered. Price turned the tiny wheel on the lantern to lengthen the wick, and the flame became strong and steady. He placed the lantern on the small wooden table beside his mother.

In the next room, Douglas muttered in his sleep.

Audrey flung herself down on the kangaroo-skin rug by the empty fireplace. She was excited about sharing the letters with Price and her mother. But not as much as usual. She couldn't stop thinking about the bushfire. Her mum hadn't said any more about it. But since they waved goodbye to Mr Akbar, she'd been jumpy and pale.

Besides that, there was a story in Jimmy's letter that bothered Audrey. She turned the sheet of paper in her hands. There was a second page still in the envelope that she wasn't going to share.

'Who's first?' Mum rested her foot on an empty wooden crate. She sat on a small armchair with a straight back. It was covered with a blanket knitted in coloured squares. 'Price?'

Jimmy had written a letter for each of them. Dougie had a drawing of a magpie and a feather. He had fallen asleep with the feather clutched in his hand.

Price sat back in Dad's battered armchair. The upholstery was faded and worn thin in places. But Dad always reckoned it was the most comfortable chair he'd ever sat in. A second lamp sat on the mantelpiece above Price's head.

He unfolded his letter. 'Jimmy says the railway line between Alice Springs and Adelaide is finished.'

Mum draped Audrey's blue smock dress across her lap and opened the tin where she kept her mending cotton and needles. 'Another reason, perhaps, that fewer camels are needed. That, and the trucks.'

Price tilted the letter so the lantern shone more brightly on the page. 'They have a thing in Adelaide called *air-conditioning*. It's a machine that blows cold air.'

'Don't the houses have windows?'

Price ignored Audrey and kept reading, 'Don Bradman got 452 runs, not out, in a cricket match in Sydney. That's the highest score anyone has ever made, in the whole world.' He refolded his letter. 'What about your letter, Mum?'

'There's a nice song that's popular at the moment called *Tip-toe thru' the tulips*. There was an orchestral concert on the radio. And Jimmy's dad is doing well in his new job.' Mrs Barlow rubbed her leg. It ached more at night. 'Anything interesting in your letter, Audrey?'

Audrey took a small white shell out of her envelope and held it out. 'It's from the beach and it smells like salt. Price, you want to smell it too?'

Price pressed his lips together. He did that when he was trying to look like a grown-up man. But Audrey thought he looked more like a boy with wind.

Mum held up a needle, squinting as she fed blue cotton through its eye.

'This is the best bit,' said Audrey. 'A man in Yass had an operation on his foot because he got a horrible weeping sore ...'

'No need to describe it,' said her mother. 'Just tell us what happened.'

'The doctor found a bullet that had been stuck in his foot for thirteen years. That bullet is older than you, Price.' Audrey looked down at Jimmy's letter again. 'A man called Francis ... C ... Ch.' She held out the first page of the letter for her mother to read.

'Chichester,' said Mum.

'That man flew from London on a moth.'

'I think Gipsy Moth might be the name of the man's plane.'

'Oh. A real moth would be better.' Audrey refolded her letter and said nothing about the second, hidden, page. She didn't want anyone else to see it.

Twenty-four

Price flung down the shovel and wiped one hand across his forehead. 'Your turn, Audrey.'

Audrey looked down at the shallow dent in the sand that was supposed to become their new dunny-hole.

Price had grunted a lot and the shovel had scraped on the hard-baked sand. But the size of the hole was disappointing.

'We're not going to finish this till Christmas.' Audrey twanged the straps of the braces which held up her loose trousers and spat on her hands, then bent to pick up the shovel. She wasn't sure why you had to spit on your hands. But Dad always did it before picking up the axe to chop wood.

Usually, Audrey liked spitting. It was fun aiming at targets. She and Stumpy sometimes had spitting competitions out in the scrub. Stumpy usually won because he had a longer neck. But spitting on her hands wasn't so much fun. Her spittle was warm and slimy.

She rested one foot on the shovel blade and leant her weight on it. It didn't go down far.

Price flumped onto the red sand and wrapped his arms around his knees.

From inside the house came the sound of a magpie. Its name was Douglas.

'I've got a question,' said Audrey.

'I know.'

Audrey stopped digging. 'How do you know? I haven't asked it yet.'

'You've always got a question.' Price

opened the water canteen and took a deep swig. A trickle ran down his chin.

'Do you think Dad's all right?' She hadn't been able to ask Mum because the look on her face was like a shut door.

''Course I do,' said Price. But his voice was too cheerful, too loud. 'He can look after himself.'

'But if the fire was that big . . .'

'There's always fires when it's dry.'

'But Mr Akbar . . .'

'Peanuts,' said Price.

Despite her worry about Dad, Audrey giggled. 'Can I ask you one more question?'

'If you keep digging.'

Audrey scraped half-heartedly at the sandy soil with the shovel. 'What will happen if Dad . . . if he doesn't come home?'

Price's bottom lip seemed to quiver. Just for a second. Then it stopped. 'I guess we'd have to grow up in a hurry.'

'Can we do that? Being a grown-up is hard. And I've still got girl things to do.'

Price shrugged. He didn't know what else to say.

Neither did Audrey.

'I've got a story to tell you.'

Twenty-five

Audrey placed both hands on the trunk of a gum tree. She put her face close to the bark and blew gently. No possum hair floated up.

'This tree is empty, Stumpy,' she said.

Months ago, an old Aboriginal woman had shown Audrey how to find possums this way. She'd shown her other things, too. But the old woman had only stayed for a few days. Visitors were like that. They popped up, then vanished. Except for Jimmy. He had stayed for a whole year. But then, he too had gone away, back to the city and his dad.

Audrey turned from the gum tree. Usually she and Stumpy had fun together in the bush. But today she wasn't in the mood for play. It was like she had an itch, but couldn't scratch it.

'No, Stumpy, we can't play hide-and-seek just now,' said Audrey. 'We have to talk about something.' She sat cross-legged on the sand. 'I've got a story to tell you. It was in Jimmy's letter.'

Stumpy reminded her how he liked stories.

Audrey wasn't sure he would like this one. She felt as though the sloshy bits in her stomach were turning cartwheels.

She looked down at the ground, not at Stumpy. 'There was this baby camel who asked his mother why he had big feet with three toes. She said it was so he could walk across sandy plains.

'Then the baby camel asked, "Why do I have these long eyelashes?"'

Audrey began tracing patterns in the red sand with one finger so she had an excuse for not watching Stumpy's expression.

'His mother told him eyelashes would keep sand out of his eyes in the desert. Then the baby camel asked why he had a hump on his back. His mum said it was for storing water when he was trekking across deserts.'

Audrey paused. She realised her pattern in the sand was close to a drawing, and that it looked a lot like Stumpy. She erased the pattern with a sweep of her hand.

'The baby camel got to thinking. He said, "I'm glad I've got big feet to stop me sinking, and long, thick eyelashes to keep sand from my eyes and that I can store water in my hump. So why are we living in a zoo?"'

Audrey sat quietly to let Stumpy think about the story. She had already been thinking about it for days. It even kept her awake at night.

In Jimmy's story, the baby camel thought

he could store water in his hump. Mr Akbar had told her that a camel's hump was full of fat. Whichever story was true, camels could certainly go for a long time without drinking water.

But the important thing about the story was that the baby camel shouldn't have been in a zoo. He should have been free to roam where he could make use of his thick eyelashes and walk a long way on his big feet.

Even Toothless, the swaggie, couldn't sleep properly in a house with a roof. He needed to breathe fresh air, feel the sun on his back, and go wherever he wanted.

Something prickled Audrey's eyes. She wiped her nose with the back of her hand. 'You're my best friend, Stumpy. But ... I want you to go away.'

Twenty-six

Audrey tried to smile, but her mouth wouldn't do it. She felt it droop at the corners.

Stumpy shook his head.

'You should be free, Stumpy. Think about Mr Akbar's camels. He let them go in the bush and they run around wherever they want. They play all the time. No one tells them what to do. You're a camel, too. You can be like that.'

Audrey listened carefully to his answer, then said, 'I know you don't like Jasmine.

Nobody does. She bites. But not all of Mr Akbar's camel are like that. It's good for camels to be free. No nose-pegs or hobbles. No bossy people.'

Audrey picked up a stick and concentrated on flicking dry leaves into the air. 'Remember Toothless? The swaggie with the sheep jaws in his bag? He said everyone should know who they are and what they want to be. Well, I think you should be free. I don't *want* you to go. But I reckon you should.'

Audrey stood up and dusted her hands on her dress. She pressed her lips together for a moment to stop them trembling. Then she said, 'I won't have so much time to play now, anyway. I might have to look after Mum some more ...' She couldn't say the words *if Dad doesn't come home.*

She listened to what Stumpy had to say, her head tilted to one side.

'I know that you don't want to leave me,' she said. 'But you have to. I can't play with you any more. You should go and do camel things from now on.'

She turned for home, her feet dragging.

Abruptly, she stopped and looked over her shoulder. 'Stop following me, Stumpy. We have to say goodbye now.'

Audrey kept walking. She knew if Stumpy saw her looking, he would follow.

Wind blew through the trees, whipping up a dust devil. It spun round and round, picking up leaves and sand. Audrey turned her face away. But the devil skidded straight past her into the bush.

She sensed that Stumpy had gone.

It paid to look where you put your feet.

Twenty-seven

Audrey opened her eyes. It was morning, but the dim light through the hessian curtain told her that it was very early.

She flexed her fingers. The blisters on her palms hurt a little. They were bigger than the dunny hole. She sighed. Her mum couldn't dig because of her leg. Douglas was too little, and busy being a magpie. So the digging was left to Audrey and Price.

Already the air was warm. Today would be another hot one. Audrey hoped Stumpy had found a cool place with lots of water.

Maybe he'd found other camels by now.

Then she heard a voice that made her heart leap. She sat up, instantly wide awake. Blisters forgotten, she thrust back the sheet and swung her legs over the side of the bed.

She checked the floor. It paid to look where you put your feet in the mornings, in case there were scorpions or centipedes.

Douglas was still asleep. His mouth hung open and there was a damp patch of dribble on his pillow.

Barefooted, Audrey shot through the lounge room and into the kitchen like a stone from a slingshot.

'Dad!'

He sat at the kitchen table, his battered old hat on the chair beside him.

'That's me.' He smiled. Wrinkles gathered around his eyes.

His hair was flattened from wearing the hat. It had been a while since his last haircut and his fair hair was shaggy. He looked thinner, and tired. His clothes were caked in dirt. He smelt like camel and sweat. His favourite pipe stuck out of his top pocket.

Audrey dashed across the kitchen and flung her arms around his neck, squeezing tight.

He hugged her back, then began to make choking noises. 'You can let go now, Two-Bob.'

She stepped back, but jiggled up and down on tiptoes. 'Mum! Dad's home.'

Mrs Barlow, already dressed and looking surprisingly awake, nodded. 'Yes, I know.'

'It's a miroolcool.'

'A miracle, is it?' Dad's eyes twinkled.

'Just like walking on a well.' Audrey once heard a story about a miracle and it had something to do with water.

With both hands, Mum carried a big bowl of porridge over to Dad.

Audrey's dad winked at her. 'This'll warm the cockles of my heart.'

Audrey scrambled onto the chair beside him.

'Mr Akbar said there was a big fire,' said Audrey. 'Bigger than the sky.'

'Well, now. That's pretty big. I saw the smoke, smelled it. But I was well clear.'

'You're smart, Dad.' Audrey rested her chin on her hands. 'How old are you?'

He blinked with surprise, then told her.

'You've been growing up for a long time, haven't you?'

He patted the top of his head. 'Matter of fact, I'm growin' right through my hair.'

Audrey sneaked a look at the bald patch on top of his head, then at his nose. There were definitely hairs growing out of Dad's nostrils, just as she told Price.

'Price and me blew up the dunny,' said Audrey.

Her dad dipped his spoon into the thick porridge. 'I thought something was missing.'

'We're digging a new dunny-hole,

though. But we reckon it might take till Christmas next year.'

'Speaking of wells,' said her mum, 'Would you mind bringing the jelly up for me, please?'

Audrey didn't mind anything this morning. Dad was home.

Still in her nightgown, she ran outside. Buttons bleated. There was a gold and red glow over the horizon.

Price rounded the back corner of the house, rubbing at his eyes.

'Dad's home, Price.'

A smile lit up her brother's face. Any trace of sleepiness vanished. He bolted for the kitchen. Audrey hadn't seen Price run that fast since a goanna mistook him for a tree and tried to run up his body to sit on his head.

Audrey looked over her shoulder. 'Last one to the well is a rotten egg . . .' she began.

But Stumpy wasn't there. Audrey was so

accustomed to him following her around that she had forgotten he'd gone.

A sad feeling swept over her. She tried to ignore it. Dad was home safe. Nothing was going to spoil a capital-letter-A day.

The well wall, made of stone and cement, was waist-high. Audrey dragged aside the sheet of iron which sat on top. When it was hot, birds would fly in to drink and then drown. The iron kept Douglas and the birds out.

Audrey fumbled with the knot in the rope that dangled into the darkness. The only way to set a jelly was to lower it at night, then bring it back up before the heat of the day melted it.

Taking care not to let go of the rope and drop the bucket, Audrey leant over the stone wall and began to pull. She breathed in the dampness of the well. It was a welcome change from the dry dustiness of the air.

She coiled the rope neatly as it grew

longer. Finally, the bucket at the end of the rope reached the top.

Audrey stared into the bucket where her mother had put the jelly bowl. 'Uh oh.'

She secured the coiled rope and replaced the iron cover on the well. Then she seized the bowl of jelly and scurried back to the kitchen.

Audrey plonked the bowl on the table and stood back. 'Cop that.'

Her parents and Price leant forward to look.

Set perfectly in jelly was a stunned-looking frog.

'Now that *is* a miroolcool,' said Audrey. 'Fair dinkum.'

Twenty-eight

Audrey sat outside the house on a kero tin watching the sun go down. She kicked at the red sand, watching it puff into a gritty cloud.

Until now, she had always thought that people were either happy or sad. They could be happy one day, but sad the next. Or happy in the morning and sad at night. But today, Audrey felt both at the same time. Happy that Dad was back. And sad that her best friend was gone.

She heard Dad's voice coming from the

kitchen. Mum laughed loudly. Dad was teasing her. Any minute, Mum would smack his arm and he would pretend to yelp. Audrey could just picture them.

Douglas squealed. He had given up being a magpie. Today he just squealed like an excited boy. Price was somewhere in the house too. Everyone was there except her. She didn't feel like company.

Dad's camels bellowed. After so many weeks with all of Dad's attention, maybe they felt left out.

Audrey nibbled the skin around her fingernail.

'So this is where you are, Two-Bob.'

Her dad came and squatted beside her. Already Mum had got to his hair with the scissors. She always fussed over him when he came home, as though he couldn't look after himself properly. Audrey wondered if she'd also snipped his nose hairs.

The light from the setting sun shone on his face, giving it a yellow glow.

'Sunset looks all the better for being home,' he said.

Audrey nodded and kept chewing at her fingernail.

'You're not thinking about putting that finger up your nose, are you? It's getting awfully close.'

She let her hand drop into her lap. ''Course not.'

He nodded. 'Want to talk about it?'

'What?'

'I might only be your dad, but I didn't come down in the last shower.'

He waited quietly for her to go on.

'Stumpy's gone,' she said.

Her dad took his pipe from his top pocket and went to put it in his mouth. He changed his mind and returned it to his pocket. 'Thought it was quiet. Where is he?'

Audrey shrugged. 'I let him go.'

Dad made a dry sound in his throat like a small cough. 'Fair dinkum?'

She told him why.

'Mmm. It's hard,' he said. 'Just like it'll be hard for your mum and me when you kids leave home. Stumpy will be all right.'

Maybe. But Audrey felt like *she* wasn't all right. What if Stumpy had forgotten her?

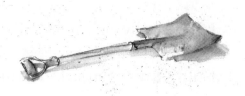

Twenty-nine

Dad looked as though he had no legs. The hole he was digging was already waist-deep. He stopped, leaned on the shovel and wiped his forehead with his sleeve.

Audrey swiped at the ground with her stick.

'I hope you and Price don't blow *this* dunny up,' said Dad. 'It's going to have real walls.'

'*Aargh*,' growled Audrey.

'What's the matter with your eye?'

Audrey screwed her left eye up even

tighter. '*Aargh*. Cut out by a sword, old fellow.'

'I thought you had something in your eye.'

'Well it ain't an eyeball, that's for sure. *Arrgh*! I'll have yer guts fer garters.'

'I wouldn't say *guts* in front of your mother. Don't reckon that's on her good-word list.' Dad resumed shovelling. 'You're a long way from the sea for a pirate.'

'I'm shipwrecked,' said Audrey.

'Hope you won't rob me.'

Audrey stopped slashing with her stick. 'I'm a kind pirate. *Aargh*. I help people.'

She relaxed her pirate's eye. It was starting to ache.

Playing games like this was usually so much fun that she never wanted to stop. A while back, when she had decided to be a dog, she had barked for three days. No words. Just panting, barking and licking. It was the licking that made her mother put her foot down. Mum didn't like having wet streaks on the back of her hand. But it had taken a whole week for Douglas to stop patting Audrey.

Today, no matter how hard she tried, being a pirate didn't seem fun. Or real. She dropped her sword-stick and turned to look out over the flat, red sand to where the scrub began. The place where she last saw Stumpy.

'What can you see out there, pirate?' Dad stretched his aching back.

'I'm not a pirate any more.'

'That was quick.'

Audrey sat on the ground beside her stick. 'It's not much fun without St . . . on my own. Price reckons he's too big for games now, and Douglas is too little.'

'You made a hard choice in letting Stumpy go,' said Dad. 'But don't grow up too quickly, Two-Bob.'

'I won't be grown-up for a long time. Maybe forever. Is forever the longest time? Or is there a bigger time?'

'Forever sounds mighty long to me.'

'Do watches make time?'

'Watches *count* time,' said Dad. 'They don't make it.'

'So where does it start?'

'Even when you're a grown-up, there are some things you just don't know.'

Audrey picked up the stick that used to be a sword and scraped it across the sand, making a wide, smooth track. 'When you were away I tried doing grown-up things like being a swaggie, a man and even a teacher.'

'I see. You were busy, then.'

'Reckon I'll stay a girl for a while.'

'I think you make a bonzer girl, Audrey.'

'But I didn't know girls could be so lonely.'

'It's not the same without you.'

Thirty

Audrey stood alone at the back of the house. She heard the crack of a ball hitting wood. Her family were out the front playing cricket.

Dad had brought home a cricket ball from Beltana, and Price had made a bat from a lump of wood. It was thicker in some spots than others. Price's woodwork was like his dad's. Solid, but crooked.

There was a shout from Dad. Douglas squealed.

Dad's dog, Grease, was barking. He didn't

like being tied to the tank stand. But if he wasn't tied, he would keep grabbing the ball in his mouth and running off with it. No one wanted to bowl when there was dog saliva all over the ball.

Audrey stared out to the edge of the scrub. The bushes seemed to blur and bend. She blinked, and the bushes looked straight again.

Running footsteps sounded behind her.

'Audrey,' yelled Price. 'We need a bowler. Want to play?'

She shook her head and kept staring at the scrubby hills where Stumpy wandered without her.

'I'll let you have a go at batting, too,' he promised. 'Mum's being the umpire cos she can't run.'

Again Audrey shook her head.

She expected Price to return to the cricket game. But he came to stand beside her. 'It's not the same without you.'

'I don't feel so good without Stumpy.'

'Yeah.' He swallowed hard, as if he wanted to say something but had to get ready first. 'Audrey, Stumpy isn't a real camel. He's imaginary.'

'No, he's not. He's just invisible. You can't see him.'

'It's awful when you miss people.' Price hesitated. 'Can I tell you a secret?'

Audrey turned to look at him. Sweat streaked the dust on her brother's cheeks. His hair was all over the place.

'When Jimmy left to go back to the city,' he said, 'I cried.'

Audrey stared in disbelief. 'I didn't see you.'

''Course not,' Price said. 'I cried by myself, when no one was looking.'

Audrey thought about that for a moment. 'How come girls are allowed to cry when people are looking, but not boys? Is that sort of like men always knowing what they're doing?'

A grin slipped across Price's face.

Audrey couldn't help chuckling.

'You're always going to remind me about blowing up the dunny, aren't you?' said Price. 'Even when we're really old and bent like boomerangs.'

'I reckon so.'

Suddenly there was a gust of wind. Red sand lifted like dry fog. Then the wind spun round and round, whipping the sand into a frenzy.

'Look at that,' said Price. 'It's a ripper.'

As soon as the words left his mouth, the wind stopped. Grains of red sand drifted back to earth.

'Whoa. That's odd.' There was a hint of awe in Price's voice.

Goosebumps ran down Audrey's arms. It was one of those ghost winds. She and Price exchanged startled glances.

Audrey gripped her brother's arm. 'If you let someone go and they come back because they want to, they can stay because you haven't made them. Right?'

'I guess so.'

'Good.' Audrey smiled. 'Because Stumpy's back. It's another miroolcool.'

She gazed towards the spot where the dust devil had vanished. 'Stumpy's running pretty fast. He'll need a drink when he gets home. Fair dinkum.'

Interesting Words

Billabong: waterhole

Billy: tin container used to boil water when camping outdoors

Bonzer: excellent, good

Bunyip: a creature in Aboriginal legends that inhabits billabongs

Chook: domestic chicken

Cooee: a call used to attract attention in the bush. It rises in pitch on the last syllable—*ee*.

Damper: a kind of bread made from flour and water, which is cooked in hot coals or ash

Dingo: Australian wild dog, often brownish-yellow with pointy ears. It doesn't bark, but howls.

Dogger:	someone who catches dingoes for payment
Dunny:	outside toilet
Dust devil:	dust caught in a whirlwind
Emu:	a tall Australian bird, which cannot fly
Fair dinkum:	true
Kick the bushes:	go to the toilet in the fresh air, usually behind a bush
Knucklebones:	animal knuckles, usually from sheep, used for playing a game
Meat safe:	a cabinet which keeps food cool. When a breeze blows through wet fabric, such as hessian, it keeps the temperature low inside the cabinet.
Ning-nong:	silly person
Quandong:	Australian native fruit, that grows on trees
Rattler:	freight train. 'Riding the rattler' meant jumping on board without a ticket, to get a free ride.

Saltbush:	a low-growing drought-resistant plant, found in the Australian bush
Scrub:	a large area that is covered with trees or shrubs, particularly in the Australian bush
Skink:	a small lizard
Smoko:	tea-break
Spinifex:	spiky grass that grows in inland Australia
Sundowner:	a bush traveller who arrives at a homestead at sundown, too late to do any work
Swag:	a bundle containing the bedding and belongings of a bush traveller
Swagman (or swaggie):	a bush traveller who carries a swag on his back, earning money from odd jobs or gifts
Three-cornered jacks:	small, hard prickles

Tickets on yourself:	conceited, thinking too much of yourself
Tucker:	food

Look out for . . .

Audrey Goes to Town

'Fair dinkum, it's a miroolcool!'

Audrey Barlow is back!

And this time she's on her way to town. It's the first time she has left her tiny Outback home and she is amazed by the shop, the pub, the houses with glass in their windows, and the wide dusty streets that actually go somewhere!

But things don't go as planned and Audrey and little Dougie are left alone with the strict and unfriendly Mrs Paterson.

Audrey has her own special way of doing things. And she does nothing by halves. When Audrey sets out to do something, she really goes to town.

Read **Audrey Goes to Town** and see how she works her magic on the people of this tiny Outback settlement.

Join . . .

The Audrey Club!

If you loved reading *Audrey of the Outback*, join Audrey's fan club to find out more!

Some Marvellous Things about The Audrey Club:

- You will receive a postcard from Audrey when you join!
- You will be the first in the WORLD to find out what happens next in Audrey and Stumpy's adventures.
- FREE updates on Audrey via *The Outback Post*.
- Enter Audrey competitions.
- FREE Audrey giveaways.
- The chance to have the author, Christine Harris, visit your school.

To join, simply send your email address to: audrey@audreyoftheoutback.com.au or send your mailing address inside an envelope to: Little Hare Books, 8/21 Mary Street, Surry Hills, NSW, 2010.

*You will need to get Mum or Dad or your guardian to send a permission note in your email or envelope!

www.audreyoftheoutback.com.au

About the Author

Christine Harris has lived in different parts of South Australia, some of them isolated country areas.

The directions to one of her houses went like this: 'the first fridge on the right, fifteen kilometres after the last pub'. Kangaroos jumped past her kitchen window, and she once found a snake skin in the shed.

She spent much of her childhood in the wild places of her imagination, as a princess in a castle, a pirate on the wild seas, an archaeologist. Even her best friend, Jennifer Hobbar, was imaginary. But Christine only realised this when she tried to visit Jennifer's house and had no idea where it was.

Christine believes the Outback draws you back to visit, again and again. She also believes that, with a vivid imagination, you can travel anywhere.

www.christineharris.com